For McKinley —

SEVEN ATE NINE!

Written By David Michael Slater

illustrated By Zachary Trover

Count on books!

magic wagon

For Emma, Elsie & Max — DMS

visit us at www.abdopublishing.com

Published by Magic Wagon, a division of the ABDO Publishing Group, 8000 West 78th Street, Edina, Minnesota, 55439.
Copyright © 2008 by Abdo Consulting Group, Inc. International copyrights reserved in all countries.

Text by David Michael Slater
Illustrations by Zachary Trover
Edited by Stephanie Hedlund
Interior layout and design by Zachary Trover
Cover design by Zachary Trover

Printed in the United States.

Library of Congress Cataloging-in-Publication Data
Slater, David Michael.
  Seven ate Nine! / by David Michael Slater ; illustrated by Zachary Trover.
    p. cm.
  Summary: When Seven eats One through Nine to become the best number, only One has the quick wit to save the
  numbers and bring the group back together again.
  ISBN 978-1-60270-012-3
  [1. Numbers, Natural--Fiction. 2. Friendship--Fiction.] I. Trover, Zachary, ill. II. Title.

PZ7.S62898Se 2007
  [E]--dc22

                              2007003793

"Me...two, three...and four...then five...and...six...um...."

One knew she could count past six. She'd done it lots of times when she was alone. But she couldn't think straight, not with everyone looking at her like that.

"You shoulda been a zero," said Seven, rolling his eyes.

"Well, I hope you don't think you're number one around here," Nine said to Seven.

"You're no hot number yourself, Nine," said Two.

Then all the numbers started squabbling
about whom was best, just like they always did.
They could be very negative numbers.

"Please stop," One pleaded, but nobody paid her any mind.

One was the loneliest number. She was the youngest and smallest, and nobody ever took her seriously. She shuffled to her hiding place and hunkered down alone, feeling too low for zero.

A while later, Nine walked by. She was all dressed up for a party with some capital letters. One watched her and wished she could go, too. That's when it happened.

It was Seven. He did a real number on Nine. He jumped out from behind a tree, opened his mouth, and swallowed her whole!

Then he ran away!

One was aghast. She saw Two, Three, and Six in the park. They were arguing over who could paint the best.

She ran over, screaming,

"Seven ate Nine!"

"Seven ate Nine!"

"Well, whoopty-doo," said Two. "Good for you."

"No! You don't understand!" One cried. "Seven ate Nine!
Seven ate Nine!"

But the numbers weren't with her. "Scram," said Six.

Five and Eight were watching Four hit golf balls. So, One ran over.

"MEEEEE!" Four yelled after whacking the ball.

"Nice shot!" said Five. "Gimme me!"

"That was a lame shot," Eight teased.
"I could do much better."

"Seven ate Nine! Seven ate Nine!" One interrupted. Then she looked back at Two, Three, and Six. They were being swallowed, too!

"Seven ate Nine!" she cried. "And Six...and...Three...and Two!"

"That's enough," said Eight. "Not even close."

"Shoo," said Four.

One scrambled back to her hiding spot. She knew exactly what she'd see when she looked back.

Seven was swallowing Four, Five, and Eight. And now he was coming her way!

"Why?" One asked when Seven found her.

"The truth, is," said Seven, "I only say I'm the best because the other numbers say they're the best. But then I realized I would be the best if I was the only one."

"But... but... I'm the only One," whispered One.

"Don't count on it," Seven said. Then he opened his mouth.

It was dark. One heard angry voices. She opened her eyes and saw all the other numbers!

"I was trying!" she said.

"We know. We know," said Six. "Seven ate Nine. We get it. Now be quiet while we figure a way out of here."

Then the numbers went back to arguing.

One grew red in the face.

She grew redder and redder and redder until she decided that once and for all, she was going to be heard. Finally, she screamed,

"WILL SOMEBODY PLEASE LISTEN TO ME!?"

One had an idea. "I need to get up to Seven's ear," she declared. "Now, everyone, stack!"

The numbers did as they were told, and One climbed all the way up.

Then she called out, as loudly as she could, "HEY!
WHY IS THAT 'L' STANDING ON ITS HEAD?"

"I'm a number, and I'll prove it!" Seven wailed, and then he spit out all the numbers.

"Uh, oh," he said when he saw how mad they were.

"We know you're not an 'L'," said One. "You're a Seven, and we appreciate you for who you are....Right?"

"Oh, all right," the other numbers grumbled.

"And no number is any better than any other,"
One declared.

"Together, we add up to a lot. Alone, none of
us are much more than nothing."

Seven looked over the numbers and then broke into tears. "I'm really sorry everybody," he sobbed.

Then all the numbers started to cry. "We're sorry we never listen to you, One," they sniffed. Then everyone cheered, "All for One and One for all!"

"We know we can count on you!" Nine added.
"Even if you couldn't count on us."

"But I can!" One protested. "Listen! Me...
two, three...and four...then five...and...six...
um... oh, no!" One was stuck again! She
couldn't think straight—not with everyone
looking at her like that.

Reading Comprehension Questions:

1. What number does One get stuck on when she is counting?

2. Where is Nine going?

3. Why does Seven eat the other numbers?

4. How does One save the day?

5. How do the numbers look at One in the end?

David Michael Slater lives and teaches seventh grade Language Arts in Portland, Oregon. He uses his talents to educate and entertain with his humorous books and informative presentations. David writes for children, young adults, and adults.

Some of his other titles include Cheese Louise, The Ring Bear (an SSLI Honor Book), and Jacques & Spock (a Children's Book of the Month Alternate Selection). More information about David and his books can be found at **www.abdopublishing.com**